Into The Sun

By
T. L. Conn

Copyright © 2023 by

T. L. Conn

Printed in the United States of America

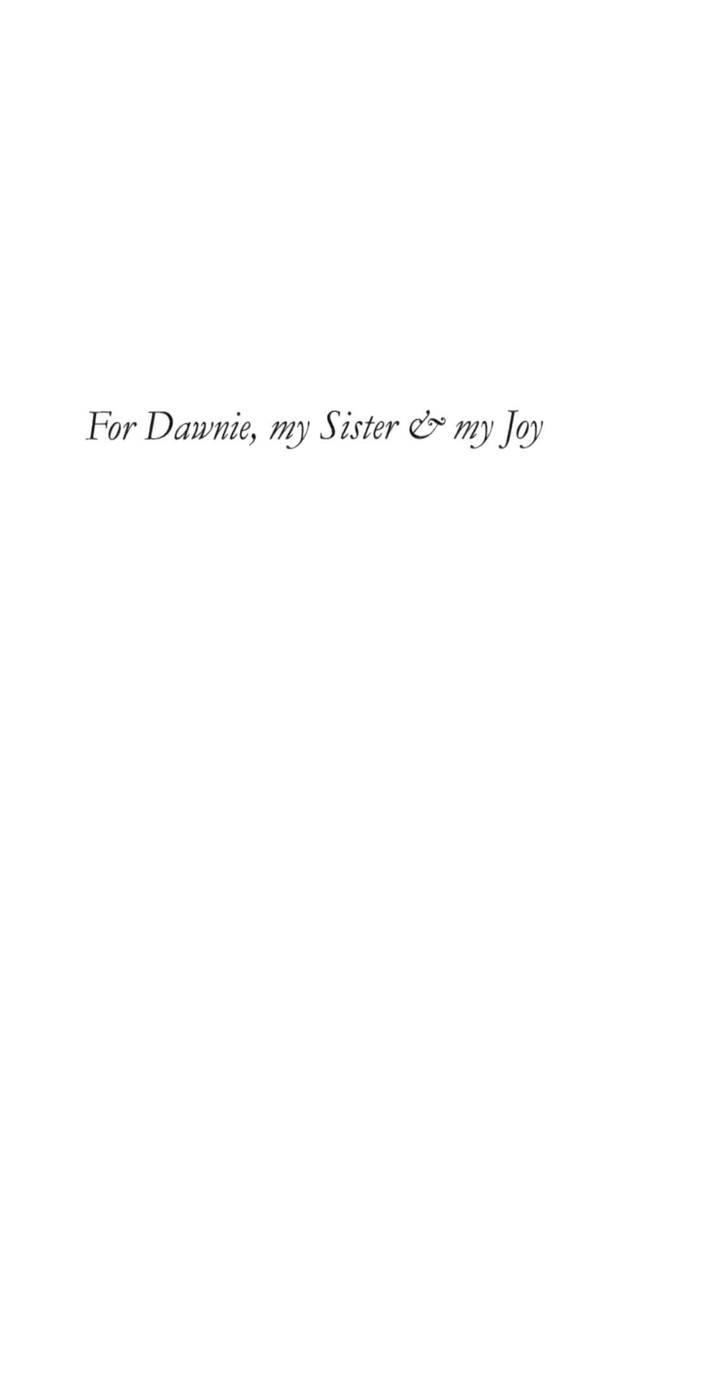

For Dawnie, my Sister & my Joy

Thank you for the inspiration, Kelly.

Table of Contents

CHAPTER 1

The day had finally arrived. Today, she would receive the university degree she had strived to achieve, a Master's Degree in Archaeology, the same degree her mother earned so many years ago at Cambridge University in London. Her mother, Margaret, had passed away ten years ago. Even so, she knew her mother's spirit was with her. She knew death itself would not keep her away.

She patiently sat in the chamber without her, waiting for the Praelector to call her name before the Vice-Chancellor.

"Most worthy Vice-Chancellor and the whole University, I present to you this woman whom I know to be suitable as much by character as by learning to proceed to the degree of Master in Archaeology; for which I pledge my faith to you and to the whole University."

The Praelector called Erica Margaret Stewart to step forward. They approached the dias and knelt before the Vice-Chancellor.

Clasping her hands, the Vice-Chancellor made the pronouncement.

"By the authority committed to me, I admit you to the degree of Master in Archaeology in the year of our Lord, 1997, in the name of the Father and of the Son and of the Holy Spirit".

Erica bowed to the Vice-Chancellor and exited through the Doctor's door of the Senate House to receive her degree certificate.

She left the university with pride of accomplishment and a strange tinge of melancholy, as she knew she would not return. It had become a home to her. Now it would become a memory.

She left London and drove to her mother's home in Warwick. It was a beautiful English home with well-kept grounds and stylish greenery. Erica would relax in her mother's study and consider her next move with her cherished degree.

She changed into comfortable clothes and went to the study where she lit the fireplace and poured a celebratory scotch for herself.

Then picking up her drink, she walked about the study, looking at her mother's photos of wonderful expeditions she led and stopped in front of her favorite photo on the wall. Her mother sat atop a camel holding her hat high in the air with an enormous smile, full of life and victorious as if she'd just ridden a bronco in an American Rodeo.

Erica lifted her drink to the photo and made a toast to her mother.

"Today is for you, Mom. Thanks for everything."

She then sat back in her mother's favorite chair and looked around the room, remembering all the precious moments she's shared with her.

Margaret, Maggie as she was known, had kept extensive records of her studies and had meticulously made notes in several journals documenting her travels. She was particularly drawn to ancient, lost civilizations. Erica was eager to follow in her mother's footsteps. She pulled down several of Maggie's journals and returned to the chair where she made herself comfortable, curled up against a large, soft pillow.

She spent the rest of the day absorbing each adventure and discovery. Reading Maggie's words gave Erica great comfort, almost as if she were sitting in the next chair, yet not quite the same as having her there in the flesh. They were a soothing proxy nonetheless.

She nibbled on English shortbread biscuits as she read along and refilled her glass twice more. Maggie's travels were always exciting and eventful, but Erica began to tire and laid the last two selections on the table next to her. She laid her head back against the chair and let herself finally relax. When she closed her eyes, flashbacks of her graduation ceremony played on in her mind.

Later, as she slowly reopened them, she noticed something odd. Maggie's library was immaculately kept; her books were always placed in alphabetical or group order by subject. What she saw seemed to be out of place. Two large encyclopedias appeared to be out of sync with a narrow piece of leather strap sandwiched between them that was slightly protruding outward.

Erica rose from the chair to investigate, and she found another journal. She deduced that this must have been intentional on Maggie's part. But why would she try to keep it out of sight? She carefully removed it and took it back to her chair, sitting down to open it. At the top of the first page was written, 'Archives of Atlantis', then the words, "It Is There —

Tell No One".

She was stunned and hesitated to read further. Maggie always detailed her expeditions meticulously. But this journal was mysterious and deliberately cautionary. Even so, Erica had the intense feeling that this was a sign from her mother. It had to be. After all these years, she had never noticed it before. But now that she had achieved her degree, she had the very true sense that Maggie was beckoning her to follow, inviting her on a fantastic journey of her own. They were both of like mind. After all, mysteries were meant to be solved.

Then, a strange memory came back to her. She remembered Maggie's return from that expedition. There had been a dramatic change in her appearance. Somehow, she had become completely gray overnight. Maggie never discussed that trip but brought back the photo.

Erica leaned back in the chair for moment and tried to piece it all together. She sat the journal down in her lap. It was quite late now and she needed to rest. She would study this journal thoroughly in the morning. She took it with her to bed and carefully tucked it under her pillow for safekeeping. It was her graduation gift.

The next day, she read through Maggie's journal while she sipped on hot tea, excitement welling up inside of her.

Maggie made several references to Edgar Casey, a gifted photographer and Sunday School Teacher. He was more notably known to thousands from all walks of life, during the early 1900s, as the "sleeping prophet". A psychic and religious seer, he unveiled the secrets of the future, and antiquity, while being in a trance or dreamlike state. His predictions concerning Atlantis were of particular interest to Maggie as he revealed the location of the hidden Archives of Atlantis. Maggie had taken a leap of faith to follow his direction and find the archives herself. And she did.

Her mother provided valuable information during her journey into the Sahara Desert and an astonishing description of her discovery. It was all there and purposely left for Erica in a safe place all these years.

Erica became wide-eyed and her breathing increased exponentially. She had to go. She simply had to find out for herself. Maggie had shown her the way, maps and coordinates all there, waiting for her.

She needed someone she could trust, someone bold enough to go with her. She knew of only one man, Grant Chandler. She picked up her phone and gave him a call.

"Grant, Erica. I found something big. We need to talk. When can we meet?"

"Hello darling, how big?" he answered

"Earth-shattering. We need to talk."

"Right," he checked his watch and continued, "can you meet me in say, an hour?"

"Yes, where? Somewhere private. Can't let this get out," she insisted.

"Is the church of St. Bartholomew the Great good for you? It should be relatively quiet at this time of day."

"It's perfect. Thanks, Grant. See you there."

Erica was so excited she could barely keep still.

Grant was waiting for her near the Priory. Erica was relieved to see that it was quiet and private, indeed. She sat down next to him and took his hand.

"Grant, Maggie found it, the greatest discovery of all time, the crown jewel."

She hesitated, almost afraid to mention it aloud even in their secluded surroundings. Grant nodded and motioned for her to continue with mouth agape with anticipation.

Finally, Erica whispered, "Atlantis".

He was overcome with the shock of what he had just heard. Finally, he urged her to go on, "The archives?"

"Yes, they are real and they are buried in the Sahara Desert. Maggie left a road map. She was there!"

"My God in Heaven!" Grant exclaimed, looking upward. He leaned closer to her. "Erica, you must go."

"Yes," she agreed with enthusiasm. "With you."

"Why, yes, what an honor you give me. Yes, I will go...we will go."

Relieved, Erica squeezed his hand and smiled broadly.

"I wouldn't want to go with anyone else."

Grant leaned back against the pew while the thought of travel plans progressed in his mind. He'd handled many expeditions in the past; travel, handlers, and funds. A professor at Cambridge himself, he knew exactly what to do to prepare.

"Yes, I will take care of all the details."

"Perfect. And remember, Grant, no one else is to know," insisted Erica. "Tell no one."

"Agreed, no worries. I'll make the arrangements."

As the days wore on, preparations were carefully and thoroughly planned to the nth degree. When all was ready, Grant met with Erica to review each leg of their journey. The exhilarating anticipation of the upcoming travel was intoxicating.

Once they were convinced all was ready, they returned home to pack and settle their affairs. There was no way of knowing how long the expedition would take or when they would return to England. With Maggie's guidance, they would succeed.

Cairo was a virtual stew of humanity, of all religious sects and beliefs. But Muslim was the most prominent. It was a bustling city of cultures, colors, and smells. A thriving, breathing entity in itself, exciting in every way, yet dangerous. Life was hard for its inhabitants. Thievery and treachery were always at the fore as their civilization clawed itself through life. Yet the history and beauty of its ancient stonework and the gracious hospitality of the people were a welcoming pleasure.

Grant and Erica checked into the hotel and went to their rooms to refresh and bathe from the journey.

They would meet in the dining room for dinner, then meet at the bar later that evening with the guide that would take them into the Sahara.

CHAPTER 2

Troy McCullum leaned back in his chair with one leg cradled on the corner of the table while he took a long drink from his glass. He would soon meet his employers at that establishment. The music was lively and he enjoyed himself while he waited.

A man and woman entered and stood at the bar. Troy was immediately taken by Erica's beauty. She was tall and slender, about 5'7 and 30 years of age, he guessed. She appeared stunning and appealing with a full mane of long, warm brown hair. He thought they must be a couple visiting Cairo on vacation. He took another drink from his glass and fantasized a romantic encounter with this woman at the bar. He just couldn't take his eyes off of her.

Then, he quickly came to his senses as the couple abruptly turned and approached his table. He put his leg down and immediately sat erect in his chair, waiting for them to speak.

"Mr, McCullum, I presume?" asked Grant.

"Yes, yes I am. Please continue," answered Troy.

"Excellent. Mr McCullum, I am Grant Chandler and this is Erica Stewart. We want to hire your services to lead us on an archaeological expedition into the Sahara to a precise map coordinate."

"Yes, of course, happy to be of service. I will guide you and the misses wherever you wish to go. I know the Sahara quite well," Troy eagerly responded.

"Thank you, Mr. McCullum. And Ms. Stewart is not my wife."

"Good to make your acquaintance, Mr. McCullum," said Erica, with a grin and flirtatious sparkle in her cool, gray eyes.

Troy's charm and manly good looks were definitely appealing to her. The moment they shook hands, a mutual attraction began to take form.

"My pleasure, Ms. Stewart," Troy grinned back at her.

"May we talk?" asked Grant.

"Yes, please," he answered, gesturing for them to sit down at the table.

Erica laid a map in front of Troy indicating the general vicinity of their destination.

"A more precise coordinate will be provided to you as we get closer to our target. How long do you believe such a journey might take, Mr. McCullum?" Erica asked.

Troy studied the map and determined the travel time to its destination, the Temples of Karnak.

"I believe this area should take about two days by camel, making camp at night for the handlers and animals to rest if we follow along the Nile. But your map shows a more westerly travel route far from the civilized roads. That will take more time traveling in the Sahara. But you can take a train and be there in a day. Why do you want my services?

"We wish to remain incognito, Mr. McCullum. The expedition is of a sensitive nature," Grant explained.

"Very well then, I'm your man. Just remember, the Sahara Desert is a fickle woman, no slight intended, Ms. Stewart. The Sahara changes from day to day, no two an alike."

"None taken, Mr. McCullum. When can we expect the journey to begin?"

"I planned everything in advance of your arrival.

We can begin tomorrow morning if you wish."

They all agreed on the next day, and each of them left the bar to retire for the evening.

By morning, Grant was extremely ill. He had been vomiting throughout the night and was convinced he had eaten something that gave him food poisoning. He was in no condition to travel but insisted Erica go on without him. He assured her that she would be in good hands with Troy McCullum. He made her promise she would journey on.

She hated the thought of leaving Grant there, sick and alone in a strange country. Even so, she gave him her promise. Grant knew she always kept her promises.

"Don't worry about me, my dear. I will be well again in a few days. Something wonderful is waiting for you in the desert. Go now."

Erica took her backpack, a bottle of water, sunglasses, and left the hotel. She met with Troy at his property where camels were waiting for her.

Troy was surprised to see Erica alone.

"And Mr. Chandler?" he asked.

"So sorry, he is not able to make the trip. Food poisoning has him flat on his back."

"How unfortunate. Is the expedition postponed?" Troy questioned.

"Not at all, Mr. McCullum; I am to leave without him. Let us proceed," she informed.

"Very well, then, you will need this."

Troy handed Erica a lightweight bundle of cloth.

"Thank you, Mr. McCullum."

"It will keep you much cooler and prevent burning."

Unfolding the bundle, Erica found a long white robe and a long white scarf.

"A scarf, in the desert?"

"Yes, it is called a Taureg. It is to protect your face and head from burning. Very important."

"Thank you for thinking of me," she said smiling sweetly at him.

Erica put on her robe and paraded around in front of him, strutting like a model on a runway, fluttering and fanning the long material about her, smiling back at him with every turn.

"Am I wearing it correctly, Mr. McCullum?"

Troy was delighted by her playful nature and smiled broadly.

"Indeed you are, Ms. Stewart."

He enjoyed the voluptuous spectacle in front of him and watched as she quickly tied back her hair, wrapping her head and neck with the Taureg.

"Ready, Mr. McCullum," Erica said, slipping on her sunglasses.

"Now then, have you ever ridden a camel, Ms. Stewart?"

"Horses, sir. Will it be similar?"

Troy chuckled and grinned at her.

"Not at all." He savored her playful pretense of ignorance. "This will be quite different."

He took her to the camel he chose for her ride and introduced her to Cleopatra.

"How wonderful it is to meet you, Your Majesty," looking back at Troy, eyes sparkling. "I hope we will become very close friends."

Troy helped Erica climb atop Cleo and said, "When she stands up, you will be very surprised. Their bodies are awkward when they get up. But they are very strong and wonderful animals. Cleo is obedient and gentle. But you need to hold on tight."

He nodded to the handler and Cleo rose from the ground throwing Erica in an unexpected forward thrust. She squealed with delight and raised her hand high into the air above her with a similar gesture Maggie had once displayed. It was an exhilarating experience. No wonder that photo in Maggie's study was her favorite.

"How thrilling," she responded. "But it's not my first Rodeo, Mr. McCullum."

"Well done, we are ready to go. Remember, Ms. Stewart, when we go into the Sahara, we go into the sun."

"Understood," Erica smiled at him. Troy was very charming and appealing.

He continued, "The Sahara is unlike any other sunlit place on earth. It is dry, searing heat during the day, not tropical and no trade winds. But the nights are cooler and less oppressive."

Troy's team of men and animals consisted of 4 handlers and 8 camels. At 7 a.m., the temperature was already climbing above 90 degrees when they set out.

Erica felt an excitement she'd never felt before. She envisioned the intrepid feeling Maggie must have felt as she began her journey, driven by a leap of faith that she would find the archives. Erica had never felt more alive than at this moment. She would rely on her mother's spirit to show her the way.

Soon, civilization faded from view as they began their trek into the desert.

The Sahara was indeed like no other place on earth. It was a sea of sand designed and defined by occasional sandstorms. Desolate, foreboding, a beautiful and deadly ocean. Travel across her waves was treacherous, slow, and demanding. Yet, navigating the mercurial peaks and valleys of her landscape was nonetheless, mesmerizing and hypnotizing.

Erica carried Maggie's compass with her at all times and checked it along the way to compare with her notes.

The day wore on at a seemingly snail's pace as the sun bore down on them. The temperature soared well over 100 degrees. Already, Erica felt drenched in sweat and breathing was difficult. The air was so dry she could barely swallow. There was not even a wisp of wind to provide relief. She was grateful for the robe and scarf Troy gave her. It helped to reflect some of the sun's ultraviolet rays and heat. Nothing here appeared to survive. Nothing at all, except her Cleo beneath her and Troy's brave and magnificent team.

Several times later in the day, she called out to Troy pointing at what she thought was a lake of water or a rippling stream in front of them. Each time, Troy had to explain they were nothing more than a mirage, an atmospheric phenomenon playing tricks with her eyes.

Each time, she was disappointed but nodded her response to his explanation. She realized that Maggie had experienced this discomfort on her journey, yet she endured. Erica was determined to do the same.

The first night they made camp, the temperature dropped dramatically and Erica welcomed the cool darkness. Troy sat next to her near a small lantern while his handlers stayed with the animals some distance away.

Erica poured some of her water on the end of her Taureg to wipe her face and neck. She moistened it again to wash her breasts. She wanted to wash away the day from her body.

Troy busied himself with selecting nourishment for them before they retired.

"Mr. McCullum, how many days did you say it would take to reach the coordinates on the map?"

"About five, Ms. Stewart."

"I see, and will every day be like today?"

"Hopefully, unless the winds kick up," he answered. He knew she was having difficulty adjusting to the harsh environment. He would keep a close eye on her.

"Thank you," she responded.

Troy handed her dates and biscuits to revive her strength and a small goat skin of liquor to enliven her spirits.

"Please drink this slowly Ms. Stewart. It is not meant to quench your thirst," said Troy.

Erica nodded and enjoyed the wonderful dates. "I believe it is time we call each other by our first names, Mr. McCullum. Clearly, we are to be close companions on this journey."

Troy was honored and smiled back at her. "Happy to meet you, Erica."

"I appreciate your company, Troy."

CHAPTER 3

They set out the next morning before dawn. But as the sun rose in the east, the day quickly progressed into another day of the same relentless and tortuous heat. Erica had nothing in her previous experiences to compare with this challenging excursion. She had only her determination and Troy's knowledge with which to rely on.

They would not make camp until sundown. Nourishment and water had to be taken en route. But Erica did not feel well this day. She was becoming weak from heat stroke and struggled to maintain her balance aboard Cleo.

Troy could see she was in distress and paused to check on her.

"Let's all stop and rest for a short while. We still have a long way to go before we reach the spring."

He reached up to her, touching her on the leg.

"Erica, are you alright?"

She tried to wipe the perspiration from her face and slowly shook her head with a negative response.

"I need to relieve myself and don't know if I can get down."

Troy gestured to a handler to make Cleo lie down. Erica was dizzy and dripping with sweat. He carefully took her off of her camel. When she reached the sand, she fell into Troy's arms, limp and listless.

He sat her down and removed her Taureg, quickly pouring water over her face and head, combing his fingers through her hair. Slowly, the water began to revive Erica and she finally opened her eyes.

"What happened? I'm so sorry, Troy. I thought I was okay."

"Have no shame, Erica. The Sahara takes what she wants. It's just a period of adjustment. You've been a real trouper, and I know you'll get through this. You have a strong mind and body; you will succeed."

She nodded back at him not completely

convinced of his words of encouragement.

"Now, step around Cleo and lean against her while you relieve yourself. She won't mind."

Soon afterward, Troy again washed her face with the water and dampened her Taureg to keep her cooler longer. Then she climbed atop Cleo, and the camel stood up again.

After everyone was ready, they continued their journey until sundown.

The handlers secured the animals and made camp. Troy joined Erica with more dates and biscuits and gave her the liquor to enliven her. The evening became cooler and Erica began to improve.

"Troy, tell me about you."

He was surprised by her question and felt a little uncomfortable.

"I would really like to get to know you better," she implored.

"Not much to tell, really."

Erica looked him in the eyes and repeated, "Why are you here? I mean, I'm grateful that you are, but what brought you into this line of work?"

"Well, my father was an Army officer, a lifer. We were stationed in Cairo before the Iraq war. He taught me all he knew about desert warfare. But when my mother died, he just gave up. I've been in Cairo ever since, didn't really have anywhere else to go."

"I'm so sorry, Troy. It's hard to lose someone you love," said Erica.

"I suppose..." then he trailed off. He'd never trusted anyone with his life's story before and he just stopped mid-sentence.

She sensed her question made him uneasy and decided to change the subject.

"Troy, this is really excellent liquor. Do they make it in Cairo?"

"Uh, no, but you can purchase it there. Quite popular among Egyptians, it's made with honey."

Erica took another sip or two while looking into the small lantern.

"Thank you for taking such good care of me today, Troy. The heat took a lot out of me and I am exhausted. I think I will retire now. I'm sure tomorrow will be more of the same."

She laid down on the blanket and quickly fell asleep.

Troy covered her with another blanket, then laid down next to her. When he closed his eyes, all he could see was Erica. He was falling in love.

When they set out the next day, clouds were gathering above them. Erica was happy to see clouds and less sun.

"A good sign, Troy?" she asked pointing to the sky. "Will it be a cooler day?"

"Maybe, but many times the clouds are followed by high winds, and that's a bad thing in the Sahara. But we must keep moving and get to the spring soon. Another day, perhaps. We need to replenish our water resources."

Erica was thankful for Cleo's slow and steady pace. She was greatly impressed by her gentle stamina and quiet obedience. No wonder camels are known as the 'ships of the desert', she thought to herself. They were tried and true, keeping a steady course, gliding through a sea of sand.

Throughout the day, clouds had hurried by causing streaks of light to pierce through their wispy veil simultaneously in many different places and easily playing tricks on the eyes. But now, something was changing. Along the horizon, the entire eastern sky seemed to blend in with the desert.

The handlers became excitable and they all pointed to the east.

"All stop!" Troy shouted. "Everyone dismount and group together!"

His handlers knew exactly what to do. The camels were made to lie down close to each other and tied together. They covered each animal's head with hoods to protect their eyes and help them breathe. A deadly haboob, a tsunami of sand and the powerful wind was barreling toward them with great speed.

The handlers grouped together lying next to the camels, strapped themselves together and covered their bodies with a large tarp used at camp. Troy and Erica joined them, strapping each other together and covering with another tarp seconds before they became engulfed by the relentless sandstorm.

The sound was horrendous and Erica thought it would never end. They were pounded by the sand. It was a terrifying onslaught.

"Stay close to me, Erica!" Troy shouted, "hold on and don't let go."

"Will it ever stop?" she cried back to him.

"Soon, soon, just keep close and hold on."

What seemed like an eternity later, it became easier to move about without being forced against the camels. Finally, when Troy knew it was safe, he lifted the tarp and stood outside. The haboob had moved on, racing to the west.

When Erica joined him outside the tarp, she threw her arms around him in a long embrace, trembling, with tears streaming down her dusty face.

"Thank you, thank you, Troy. I was so frightened."

He comforted her and said, "I'm proud of you. You were very brave."

He wiped away her tears and handed her water to wash away the dust from her face and quench her thirst.

Upon inspection, all of Troy's men and camels had survived the ordeal. They refreshed themselves and gave water to the camels. Although the sandstorm demanded the use of more of their water resources, Troy's careful planning would be enough to get them to the spring.

After they had a short time to regroup and repack the animals, they remounted and continued on their journey.

The rest of the day was like the day before, sun

and heat, heat and sun. The wind had completely stopped and the hours wore on until the light of day began to fade. Erica was relieved to feel the temperature drop. She was eager to rest.

At camp that night, Troy and Erica again sat together enjoying their meager meal and the honey liquor.

"How many more days before we reach the coordinates, I showed you?" Erica asked.

"Two, may three. We should reach the spring before end of the day tomorrow."

"Water, how wonderful. I so look forward to it. Do sandstorms, haboobs, you call them, occur often, Troy?"

"They can be frequent this time of year. The Sahara is always a formidable opponent. She is not for the faint of heart," he answered.

"Yes, indeed. I knew this expedition would not be easy, but not as lethal as it was today."

"You mean you do not have haboobs in London?" he asked with a twinkle in his eye.

Erica broke into laughter and flashed a brilliant smile. Troy returned her smile with a grin. It was wonderful to see her light up.

"How positively absurd," she responded to his preposterous jest. "No, of course not, not at all. England is green. But of course you know that, don't you? Why Mr. McCullum, I believe you are toying with me."

"I am, and I am enjoying it," Troy admitted with a huge grin. "Anything to see your smile."

Erica's inner desires rushed over her as they looked into each other's eyes. She had a tremendous urge to simply fall into his arms and give herself up to him. What she felt deep inside was real, undeniable and unstoppable. But she maintained her composure. It had become evident that their attraction to each other would result into something much more, and Troy's response was validation of that certain outcome. It was just a matter of time.

"Let us turn in early tonight and leave earlier in the morning. We can travel more easily without the sun," Troy suggested.

"Yes, I am more than ready. What a day it has been."

Erica stood and touched Troy on the shoulder. "Thank you again for keeping me and everyone else safe. You are my hero."

"My pleasure, Erica; a very good night to you."

She sweetly smiled to him and laid down on the blanket. As she drifted off to sleep, romantic visions of Troy and making love began to fill her mind with possibilities.

CHAPTER 4

Under the dark and cool early dawn, the party regained the journey.

As morning sun rose on the horizon, a splendid sky of pastel hues streaked across the desert giving Erica a renewed sense that the promise of something wonderful was yet to come.

She felt more alive today. Cleo kept her steady and even pace while soft, white clouds slowly rolled along. They were not the angry clouds of yesterday; they were billowy and tall, now and then even providing shade from the sun.

Erica checked her compass and Maggie's notes while the pleasant jingle of melodic bells, chimes, and trinkets played merrily around the necks of the camels. She wondered why she hadn't noticed them before.

Even the air felt different today, somehow cooler and easier to breathe. As the hours passed during their travel, Troy and Erica kept frequent eye contact. She loved the attention he gave to her and admired his strong and viral body.

Much later in the day, Erica saw what she believed might be water on the horizon and shouted out to Troy, "Another mirage?"

"No, he answered back. This time it's real."

Troy told everyone to stop; then he sent one of his men to scout out the spring. He wanted to make sure it was safe enough for Erica.

They waited, grouped together for his man to return while the camels began grunting and talking to each other.

"What are they doing, Troy?"

"They know there is water ahead. But we must be certain it is safe to approach it. Many caravans come to this spring. Some are nomads with women and children; others might be of a very different sort, bandits and thieves. They must not know we have a woman with us."

Erica was startled to learn of this danger yet

humbled and grateful that Troy's main concern was her safety. He could see she had become quite troubled.

"Erica, we will take care of you. I will not let you go in harm's way. Trust me."

She silently nodded back to him, but worry was still etched across her face.

Soon, Troy's man returned to the group with good news. No one was at the spring. It was safe for them to go.

In an attempt to cheer her, Troy said, "When we reach the spring, the water is all yours. You can bathe and refresh yourself. We will take the animals to the other end of the oasis pool to water them. It will be private for you."

"Thank you, that you so much. I really appreciate it, Troy. I can't wait to bathe," she said putting on a brave smile.

Troy gave the order for his team to proceed to the spring. The oasis was a jewel in the desert. Palm trees and the small bushes lining the pool thrived at the water.

After they arrived, Erica walked into the pool fully clothed in an attempt to clean them as well. Then she completely disrobed, tossing her wet clothing on a nearby bush to dry. She laid herself into the pool letting her hair and body drink in the life-giving water. She almost felt reborn, as if baptized by nature itself.

The sun was still above the horizon. It would help her body and hair dry before dressing. She'd purchased a lovely, dark, Kaftan dress in Cairo that freely flowed to her ankles. The deep vee neckline was beautifully embroidered with many colors. She was eager to wear it that night for Troy.

When she stepped out of the water, she sensed she was being watched. Even so, she continued to stand in the remaining sunlight.

Troy had come to check on her, but he instantly froze when he saw her come out of the water and didn't make a sound. The water glistened over her full and voluptuous breasts while her long hair draped down her back. Completely nude, she was incredibly fit and toned. He couldn't make himself speak in the presence of such beauty. She was a Goddess.

In a few moments, the warm air dried the moisture from Erica's body. She stepped into her sandals, then slowly raised her arms above her head slipping on the beautiful dress, wearing nothing else underneath. It gently cascaded down the length of her body to her ankles.

She knew Troy was there. She had become accustomed to the sound of his footfall. The handlers shuffled when they walked. But Troy's steps were heavier and definite. Still, she allowed him to see her without acknowledging his presence. It was a delicious feeling.

Once she dressed and began gathering her travel clothes, Troy cleared his throat and noisily approached the pool.

"The camels have been watered and camp is almost ready. Did you enjoy the spring, Erica?"

"Yes, it was wonderful and so invigorating," she replied with a grin.

Her hair had become almost dry, freely moving about her shoulders.

"You look stunning this evening, Ms. Stewart. A new dress?" he asked smiling back at her.

"Yes, I'm so glad you like it." She flashed a beautiful smile and continued, "the water is all yours. See you back at camp."

She left Troy standing at the pool. He clearly appeared mesmerized.

When Troy returned to camp, he looked

refreshed with the dust washed away from his handsome face.

They ate their meal together in the cool evening air enjoying each other's company.

"You said we should reach the coordinates on the map in a day or so?" she questioned.

"Yes, hopefully we will, but the sandstorm slowed us down some. Erica, I have been to that location before. There is nothing there. What are we looking for?" he responded.

"The archives of Atlantis, Troy. A pyramid structure of some kind exists at these coordinates. And I want to find it. My mother was also an archaeologist. She was there several years ago and found it using the information provided in the readings of Edgar Casey. I have her journal; the coordinates are here." she showed him the map.

"I've heard of this Casey. These coordinates on your mother's map appear to be much further west of Luxor and the Valley of the Kings."

"Precisely, Troy, the early Egyptians were refugees. Their ancestors were Atlanteans who survived the great upheaval and migrated to the land of Egypt. Atlanteans were a highly advanced civilization, much as we are today, and perhaps more so. But their reckless handling of nuclear energy brought on terrible volcanic action that tilted the earth on its axis. The north and south poles of today were once tropical and life flourished. But the devastation destroyed Atlantis, sinking it into the Atlantic Ocean for tens of thousands of years. Entire continents were reconfigured.

As they began their reconstruction period in Egypt, they brought their technology with them and built pyramids and a structure to house their history their archives. The archives were not intentionally buried or hidden at all. In fact, they visited often. But after the final upheaval, the climate and repositioning of the former land masses were destroyed so violently Egypt's fertile and green land became a dead zone. A great desert was left behind. The volcanic eruptions created terrible destruction and atmospheric climate change worldwide. What was once cold became tropical, what was once tropical became frozen tundra."

"What you're telling me is amazing, Erica. I've heard many theories, but yours makes more sense. I believe you." said Troy. "If it really does exist, you can trust me to get you there."

"Thank you, Troy." She continued, "Luxor and Cairo's pyramids, along with the Sphinx, were finally discovered in the modern age. Archaeological finds are being unearthed and documented all the time. A truly golden age of discovery has been upon us," she sweetly smiled at him.

Troy enjoyed her excitement and smiled back at her, gently touching her face. "I will help you in every way you ask. I am at your service, madam."

In the dim light of their small lantern, their moment suddenly presented itself, and their passion became too powerful for them to ignore. They kissed and held each other in a long embrace. Without taking his eyes off of her, Troy turned off the lantern and carried her to the waiting blanket close by.

Erica was more than willing. After they disrobed, Erica laid on her back and gave herself to him. Troy kissed and stroked her body, exploring every inch of her. She immediately reacted to his touch as he pleasured her, breathing out long, deep sighs of ecstasy and undulating her pelvis while she surged again and again. Troy pleasured Erica more than an hour as she laid completely enraptured, her body begging for more.

Periodically, she opened her eyes, looking at the crystal-clear sky. The Milky Way had positioned itself directly above them while the stars and planets twinkled from horizon to horizon. The enormity of its splendor took Erica's breath away. She felt enraptured in a way she'd never felt before, engulfed in the deepest ecstasy, with a joy so complete it was difficult to comprehend. The night sky was alive with shooting stars in all directions so close she could almost touch them. It was a living, breathing entity of spectacular beauty. She was no longer just herself but becoming one with desire and the universe. Tears of great joy streamed down the side of her face.

When Troy finally paused, she rolled him onto his back, and straddled atop him, allowing him to penetrate her. She slowly and rhythmically moved her hips as his pelvis rose repeatedly to meet hers and sighed with pleasure while he caressed her breasts. Moments later, she laid herself on top of his chest and kissed his neck, sighing softly into his ear.

He then gently rolled her onto her back again and made deep, sensual love to her until they reached their climactic bliss together. They panted as they caught their breath and would have continued their lovemaking long into the night, but Troy could see that the heat of the day had finally brought on exhaustion. Erica closed her eyes and fell fast asleep. Her face was beautiful and serene under the starlight.

Troy lovingly covered her nakedness with a blanket and laid down next to her until early dawn.

He had fallen madly in love with her.

Before morning's light, Troy woke Erica.

"Good morning; how did you sleep?" he asked.

She smiled at him. "Better than I have in years. Thank you,"

"You were incredible last night, the Queen of Egypt, Goddess of Love," he grinned down at her.

She cupped his face in her hand and replied, "Give yourself some credit, Pharaoh; you were a lion, my King."

She wrapped her arms around him, pulling him toward her, and they kissed.

"My team will be coming soon. We need to prepare and pack," said Troy.

"Yes, but I would like to bathe first."

"I will join you," he quickly responded.

They walked into the pool together and bathed themselves in the cool water. When finished, they held each other close once more, enjoying their nakedness in a long embrace before leaving the spring. After they dressed, they walked back to camp for morning nourishment.

They were both quite famished and sat down for a moment to gleefully devour their dates, biscuits, and water.

By the time they finished packing up their camp, the handlers and camels joined them. They all mounted up and headed out into the cool morning light. The merry jingle of the trinkets around the camel's necks had new meaning for Erica. She was happy, fulfilled, and felt a great sense of promise of the discovery that lay ahead.

CHAPTER 5

The map coordinates indicated a location far outside of Abydos and the Valley of the Kings, away from civilization and Nile traffic. As did Maggie, Erica did not want anyone to know where they were going. Secrecy was imperative, and she didn't want to draw any attention to their purpose. Even so, they were getting close now and had to turn east toward the Nile.

The day's travel was hot and there was not a breath of wind. Along the way, they saw a caravan in the distance headed away from the Luxor region. Strangely, another followed with the hour. Seeing one caravan in this area was improbable, but two in such a short time was unusual and Troy became concerned.

When the third caravan appeared, Troy decided it was wise to send a rider out to talk to them. He held Erica and his team in place while they waited for his man's return.

Erica busied herself with Maggie's compass and journal notes while she stayed aboard Cleo. Troy and the others dismounted to relieve themselves and walk about to stretch their legs.

"What do you think is happening, Troy?" Erica asked.

"Don't know, but it doesn't feel right."

Before long, his man rode back to the others and dismounted. Troy talked to him while his man excitedly pointed in the direction of Luxor. When finished, he walked up to Erica shaking his head, glancing to the east.

"So, what he tells me is that there has been a terrible attack at the Temple of Hatshepsut. Says over 60 people were gunned down and killed, most of them tourists. It was a bloody massacre."

"But who, who did this? Why?" Erica questioned, completely shocked by the horrible news.

"He says he doesn't know for sure, but Islamist rebels are always fighting Egypt's government, always fighting for control. He says the people with the caravans do not feel safe in Thebes. They want to take their goods to market in Cairo but bypass the violence, far away from the main routes. No one is safe there now."

Troy became increasingly worried about Erica's safety. She was visibly shaken by this terrible news.

"I think we need to stop for the day and camp right here for the night."

He told one of his men to help Erica dismount and told his men to set up camp. There would be no lights in the camp that night. He instructed his men to arm themselves, maintain minimal noise levels, stand guard in shifts, two men at a time and to protect the camp at all costs. They quickly complied.

Erica was terribly concerned, "You are so worried, Troy. Will we be alright?"

"Too many of these caravans carry thieves, kidnappers, very bad men," he answered.

"Kidnappers?" she repeated. "Why would they kidnap?"

"Erica, you're a beautiful woman. They can take you and sell you for sex. Trust me."

She gulped and meekly responded, "Whatever you say, Troy. Thank you."

He kissed her on her forehead and gave her a hug. "It will be okay."

While they camped, Erica ate her meal alone.

Troy came and went, armed with a sidearm and carried a canteen of water. At one point, he joined her when he thought it was safe enough.

He sat down next to her and put his arm around her shoulders. "We will keep you safe. Are you alright now?"

"Not having as much fun tonight as last night, that's a certainty."

She let out a nervous chuckle, and Troy kissed her on the cheek.

"Erica, have you ever shot a gun?" he asked, showing her his revolver.

"The closest I got to weapons was fencing in College. Guns weren't a prerequisite for a Masters in Archaeology at Cambridge. So it wasn't part of the curriculum," she said, managing a grin.

"I'm sure it wasn't, Ms. Stewart," he said, grinning back at her. "But let me show you the safety features just in case, alright? Trust me?"

"Yes, absolutely," she answered.

Soon afterward, Troy rejoined his men. The night was long. He would keep his vigil.

The next morning, Erica studied Maggie's journal again and again, looking for some indication of where to look for the archives. She'd read it a hundred times but couldn't shake the feeling that she was missing something. She knew Maggie was meticulous in her detail. It simply had to be there...perhaps in plain sight.

Frustrated, she laid the journal down in her lap and ate her morning nourishment of endless dates and biscuits, dreaming of golden fish and chips with ice-cold ale in Cambridge. But soon enough, she thought to herself. She was living the most exciting experience of her life and was grateful to be where she was. She would return to England soon enough.

The night's vigilance was successful, and Troy joined her for breakfast. In between shifts, he had managed a little shuteye and would be good to go on when they broke camp.

"I missed you last night," said Erica.

"So did I. You don't know how much I wanted to be with you," Troy responded.

"Troy, you know this region very well. My mother's journal says the archives are close, but at what precise coordinate? I'm missing something. She would have marked it on the map, somehow. Perhaps a small notation, a symbol, a misspelled word or group of words, but I can't seem to find it.

Sometimes, when you're so close to something, you can't see the forest for the trees."

She handed him Maggie's map. "I need fresh eyes. What do you see, Troy?"

He silently looked the map over, turning it on its side once or twice. Then he called off each of the Temples of Karnak, one by one. He noticed Maggie made notations along the higher ground, in particular, at the cliffs of Deir el-Bahari and the nearby Valley of the Kings. The cliffs encircled the Temple of Hatshepsut. The Valley of the Kings was encased in over 1,000 feet of limestone and other sedimentary rock, but there was a strange mark on the western side of the cliffs where the wall reached its highest elevation. A puzzled looked crossed Troy's face as he contemplated this mark.

"What's this? Why would she make a mark here? There are no temples on this side of Deir el-Bahari," he said aloud.

He handed Maggie's map back to Erica, pointing out the mark he found.

She wondered if the mark was simply a mistake and looked closer. Maggie had marked each of the temples west of the Nile with a roman numeral in their order of location from north to south instead of using the letters of their names. She gave Abydos the number I, Ramses II was numeral VII. But why would she number them?

"I'm just not sure about any of this, Troy. It looks like 2, 3, and 4 are almost on top of each other." Erica was quite perplexed and started counting the temples on her fingers.

Suddenly, a strange look came across Troy's face. "Erica, how many temples have been discovered along the Nile near Thebes?"

"Easy, eight. And so?" she questioned.

"And how many are on the west bank?"

"Six," she answered with a smile.

Troy cocked his head and continued, "So, why would Maggie give the Temple of Ramses II a number 7?"

Erica looked as if a light bulb suddenly lit up. "Of course! Does this mark near the wall look like a III to you?"

Troy looked again and turned the map to its side. "It does if you look at it sideways."

"Excellent, Troy!" She gave him a hug and a big kiss with a huge smile.

He hugged her back, just as excited as she was.

Then they hugged again.

"So, we go to the western side of the cliffs. We go to the number 3 marker. Do you think it will be safe enough after the shootings?"

"It's hard to say for certain. There is always so much unrest in the land of Egypt."

They set out with caution and slowly headed east for Deir el-Bahari. No other caravans or traffic of any kind had been sighted the night before or that morning. Yet, Troy was uneasy about terrorist activity that may still exist in the region, even though he was confident that the temples were being heavily guarded by government soldiers.

Several hours later, they could see the massive limestone cliffs in the distance. The terrain was impressive from that view. Erica knew instinctively that it was the right place. Maggie was here. But by now, most of the day was already spent.

Troy stopped the team and they all dismounted for water and relief. Erica could see that finding the exact location of the archives was an insurmountable task, like finding a needle in a haystack. There were no road signs to point the way; in fact, they were playing three-dimensional chess and needed a strategy. How high, how low do they search? Somehow, she knew in her heart that Maggie would give her a sign. She didn't bring her daughter this far to disappoint. Erica would rely on her intuition and knowledge. It was here. They just had to look closely, and she knew Troy would know how to help her.

Troy handed her his binoculars. "Take a closer look from here. You won't get a better view."

"Thank you."

"It will be sundown soon; we may as well make camp for the night and start out fresh in the morning."

"Yes, good idea. We need to think this through."

They made camp and sat together by a small lantern while they ate and drank the honey liquor.

"Troy, I need to share my feelings with you. As excited as I am to discover the archives, I also have a reservation as to its anonymity. Perhaps the archives is something that should be left unseen, undiscovered. Maggie returned older than her years. She wrote, "Tell no one" on her journal. Why am I suddenly so apprehensive? I value your thoughts; please speak freely."

He softly rubbed her back and kissed her cheek.

"It will pass. I believe we are all here for a reason, in this place, in this time. We are here to experience what we are meant to do, be who we are meant to be."

Erica snuggled close to him and put her arm around his waist.

"I will be with you," Troy continued. "We will do this together. I am with you all the way."

She let out a heavy sigh and leaned into his arms.

"Let's lay down now. I will make you feel better," he promised.

They kissed and turned off the lantern.

CHAPTER 6

By morning, Erica did indeed feel better. She felt refreshed and renewed, ready to explore. Her night with Troy was filled with lust and love. They had become more than lovers; they had fallen in love. He softly kissed her awake and gently caressed her body under the last of the night's brilliant stars. One by one, they blinked out, leaving the morning star above the eastern horizon, just above the glow of morning's light. It illuminated the limestone, in the distance, in such a way as to define each crevasse and wind-eroded indentation.

Troy continued to stroke her body while she turned her gaze to the beauty that loomed in the east. She had the feeling that the intricate designs were almost speaking to her. Then a pattern began to emerge, like faint hieroglyphics on the temple walls. One pattern oddly resembled two parallel columns with a hint of a carving in between them.

"Troy, wait a moment, love. Please look at that shadow on the cliffs below the morning star, and tell me what you see."

"I don't see anything but you," he answered.

"Please, stop a minute and look at the formations on the cliffs. It's about 100 feet up from the desert floor and just left of center."

He brushed his hair back from his face to accommodate her and rubbed his eyes. "Okay."

Erica pointed toward the limestone and waited for his response.

"I see shadows carved into the rock," he said.

"Do you see what looks like columns?"

"Hard to tell," he replied.

"Troy, please look again," she implored.

After a brief hesitation he said, "Yes, I think I see it. Doesn't look like a natural formation, it's more like something cut into the wall."

Erica gave him a huge kiss and exclaimed, "Yes! I believe it is obscured and faded during the daylight because it is so faint."

Then, within seconds, the sun peaked over the

horizon and the shadow disappeared.

"Troy, I think it is there! The archives is there."

"So do I. Erica, I know you are excited, but let's take this slow. We'll maintain camp here and ride to the limestone for a closer look," he suggested. "We must continue to use caution."

Erica nodded and said, "Agreed."

When they were ready, they were accompanied by two of Troy's men. Two stayed behind with the animals.

As they approached the limestone, Erica became somewhat confused by its appearance. What she saw now looked nothing like it did that morning before sunrise. The land mass blended together as all one color with the sun glaring off its light tan surface. She was certain she saw columns, but where were they now?

She shook her head in disbelief. "Where are the columns?"

Troy felt her disappointment and tried to soften her discouragement.

"We saw them together. Whatever you decide, I am at your service."

Erica blew Troy a kiss and continued her search. After a while, a ledge of some kind began to take shape above them as the sun reached its highest point.

"Limestone is always tricky. It changes continually as the sun moves across the sky," offered Troy.

"Indeed, it does. Excellent camouflage, and perhaps intentional. The Atlanteans were extremely advanced; they knew what they were doing to preserve this place."

She touched the surface of the limestone, amazed by its softness. It looked so strong from a distance. The compaction of settling sediment throughout millennia provided some strength, yet they would still need to take care, stepping wisely to prevent breakage or cascading rockfall.

"Well then, this will take some time," said Erica.

"I am willing and able, love," said Troy. "The longer I can be with you, the better.

"Let's build a marker with a few stones. It will be easier to find again later. Then we need to find a way up to that ledge and see where it leads."

Together, they built the marker, then stepped back a few feet to get a better view of the ledge above them. There had to be a way to get to it. But wind erosion had made it difficult and far more treacherous. They each walked along the base of the limestone in different directions looking for an access route. All they really needed was a safe path of some kind, but neither could find a way high enough to reach the ledge.

"Maybe we should move further to the side to see what possibilities that might offer."

"Yes, let's step back again and look for a way..." Troy was cut short when one of his men began yelling and excitedly pointed to the south.

A vehicle was fast approaching, kicking up sand dust all around it.

"Erica, cover your face. I don't want them to know you're a woman."

She quickly wrapped her head tighter with the Taureg and put on her sunglasses. Troy wished he had all his men with him. They were seasoned fighters, and five men were better than three.

"When they get here, Erica, stand to the side with the other men and don't speak."

"Whatever you say."

They all waited next to the camels and stayed silent. Soon, the vehicle slowed and came to a stop.

Troy was relieved to see it was a government vehicle, and the six men riding inside were dressed in military uniforms.

He left the others by the camels and walked up to them to talk.

One of the men sitting in the passenger side of the vehicle questioned Troy's reason to be there, as well as the traveler with him.

"This is my party. I have papers."

Troy handed him his identification and the government permits that he carried in his shirt pocket, then stood back waiting for a reply.

Erica heard the muffled conversation and one of the soldiers pointed to an area some distance away. Then they ended their meeting amicably with a wave. The vehicle turned around and headed back to the south.

"Everything is okay. They are on patrol, questioning everyone in the region in an effort to keep it safe from further terrorist action," Troy informed.

He saw tremendous relief on Erica's face as soon as she removed her glasses and pulled down the Taureg.

He put his arms around her and continued, "We're okay. They have everything under control."

Erica sighed and said, "Thank you, Troy."

He held her closely for a long time. Then he gave her a big smile.

"I think the soldiers showed us way up the limestone to the ledge. We need to move farther to the north and then walk back toward our marker. They said there is easier access to the hillside there. But it is a great distance."

Erica hugged him even stronger. She was overjoyed with his news. Beaming, she said, "Let's go."

They set out to the north several kilometers searching for a slope of some kind that would gently take them to the elevation they needed. But it was illusive and soon hours passed by without success.

"Troy, do you think the soldiers understood you? The sun has already reached the western sky. How long will it take us to get back to camp?"

"Hopefully, we will get back by nightfall taking a straight route. But let's stop a moment and watch what the sun does to the limestone. You've given me an idea," he responded.

As they sat atop their camels facing the east, they watched the sun dance along the cliffs. Shadows came and went changing the colors of the sediment. Then, within the hour, a slope amazingly began to appear where before it had been obscured by the sun's glare.

"Yes!" exclaimed Erica. Troy, you're brilliant."

"Thanks, but it was really your idea. I just listened to what you said," he grinned back at her. Let's build a marker for tomorrow, then head back to camp."

As soon as they reached camp, Erica took her canteen and cleaned her body as best as she could, letting down her hair. Remembering the cool oasis pool, she wished she could have cleaned herself better. Yet, slipping on her Kaftan dress would at least help to cool her down more quickly. Besides, she knew Troy loved to see her wearing it, at least for a little while.

She joined him by the lantern, then they ate their meal and drank the honey liquor together. Troy's charm and good nature were always enjoyable.

"You know, I think you would love the wonderful cuisine we have in London. Have you ever been there?" Erica asked.

He shook his head and said, "Many places around the world, but never England."

"I understand," she responded with a nod. "Many adventures, I'm sure. I would love to show you my country someday."

Troy smiled back at her. "Let's turn in now. Tomorrow will be a very long day."

"Yes, let's," she agreed, eager for the night's pleasures that were sure to come.

Troy turned off the lamp and together they went to the waiting blanket. They embraced and kissed while he slowly removed her dress. He kissed her body and pleasured her until they made love under the brilliant canopy of sparkling stars, then they finally fell asleep in each other's arms.

As morning came to light, they laid together observing the shadows on the limestone hillside. Again, fleetingly, the columns appeared, then vanished as the sun rose higher in the east.

Erica felt excitement well up inside of her. She knew the day's investigation would take them closer to the prize. She cleaned herself while Troy dressed and prepared morning nourishment, gathering fresh canteens of water to take with them.

After she dressed in her travel clothes, she put on the robe and gathered her Taureg. Then she joined Troy for breakfast.

"You were amazing last night, Erica," said Troy, smiling at her.

"We work well together, don't we?"

"Hell yes." He leaned toward her and kissed her cheek.

"How long do you think it will take us to reach the ledge?" she asked, chewing on a date.

"Hard to say. To reach the slope may take close to an hour. Tracking back to the location of the first marker will take considerable time. The trek will be precarious at best since limestone is so unpredictable. We need to take it slow and keep close," he answered. "Then we need to search for the columns. If it is what you are looking for, it will take time to study. We won't know what to expect until we encounter it."

"Right, let's get started," Erica agreed.

CHAPTER 7

Troy's estimation of time was nearly accurate. Once they reached the second marker, they dismounted and put on backpacks to carry their essentials with them. They would need both hands and a steady balance to traverse the limestone.

He told his men to ride along with them, following their progress on the hill, and keep them in sight at all times.

It was, as it was every day, hot and the glaring sun distorted their path as it reflected off the limestone. As promised, it was extremely difficult to stay surefooted. What looked like powder was more sedimentary, and what appeared solid gave way easily. Even though they tried to keep an even pace and a straight path, they were repeatedly forced to try a different tack around several sections of sediment that prevented forward motion.

After two hours, Troy called Erica to stop and rest. She gladly complied and sat down on the most solid surface she could find. He sat down next to her and they drank their water.

"Are you okay?" he asked.

She wiped her face with the end of her Taureg and nodded back to him, taking another drink from her canteen. She looked back at him, shaking her head.

"You were right; this limestone is a bitch," she complained.

Troy didn't expect her remark and looked surprised. When she saw his reaction, they both began chuckling together.

"I absolutely agree. As I said, the Sahara is a woman of many moods."

She lifted her canteen to him as if giving a toast, then wiped her face again.

"Do you think we will reach the first marker soon?"

"Yes, soon, now."

Erica watched as his men and the camels came to a stop at the base of the hill. Cleo suddenly cried out and looked up at her.

"Troy, poor Cleo. She looks so lonesome."

He smiled at her and said, "She does. I believe she loves you; who wouldn't?"

Erica softly smiled and cradled Troy's face in the palm of her hand. "You are so very sweet, Troy. I'm so happy we are on this adventure together."

"Wouldn't miss it for the world." He looked to the sky to determine how much daylight they still had. "Right, perhaps we should get going again. The sun is on the move. Ready?" Troy asked.

She took another drink and said, "Ready."

They secured their canteens in their backpacks and Troy helped her to get to her feet.

Again, they continued along the cliffs for another hour in the worst heat of the day. Erica lost her balance more than once but managed to stay upright. The sun was blaring and relentlessly searing hot.

Just as Erica thought she would faint, she saw someone below waving some kind of flag or cloth, and she focused her sight on him to maintain her senses. One of Troy's men had ridden ahead to the first marker to help signal its location.

Troy came up right behind her and steadied her balance, tightly holding his hands around her waist.

"Do you see him?" she asked.

"Yes, he's real; he is with us. He is showing us the marker. We are here," he told her.

"Thank you, thank you," she whispered.

"Let's sit again and have some water."

They sat down together and Troy pulled the Taureg away from her face and head. He poured water from his canteen over her head and watched closely until she began to recover from heat exhaustion.

"Thank you, Troy. Did you say we are here?"

"Yes, this is the place where we saw the ledge. It is here. I believe we are sitting on it. The columns must be close as well," he nodded with encouragement.

Erica tightly held his forearm filled with excitement and broadly smiled back at him. She brushed the hair away from her face and prepared to stand.

"Okay, I'm good now. Let's go again."

Troy stood up with her to made sure she was able to continue on her own before he let go of her.

They then walked along the ledge to a place of high cliffs. Erica knew she would need to study the facade closely for any indication of carving or cutting into the surface. She touched the stone as she moved next to the wall.

Amazingly, form and design began to reveal themselves, extremely subtle, but something was definitely there. As she ran her hand along the formations, an intense thrill leaped into her breast that she hadn't felt since she was a child, opening the most wished-for gift on Christmas day.

She believed she was standing in the exact place as her mother so long ago. She was here, and the archives had to be here. Erica studied the rounded stonework and looked for the other column. She knew it had to be only a few feet away. Walking a little further to the right, she realized she was standing in between them.

"Troy, this is it. We are here. Do you see anything that looks like a carving above us?"

"No, I think you are looking at it. It's right in front of you. Do you see the triangle?"

"Yes, I see it now."

She ran her right hand against the area brushing away the dust lodged in its indentations to get a closer look...and then an odd sensation befell her as she began to disappear. Troy quickly grabbed her arm and immediately felt lightheaded.

The experience was euphoric and dizzying, but they found themselves standing together inside some kind of chamber. They were, indeed, inside the hill, in a chamber lit by a source they could not define. The domain was immaculate and pristine. It looked like some kind of laboratory with what appeared to be a computer mainframe.

"My God! Troy, we're here and we're alive!" Erica exclaimed wide-eyed. "How did we get here? Okay, let's take time to analyze this. Let's just breathe...wait, there is air in here. How?"

They held each other, side-by-side and silently began to observe their surroundings. The chamber was immaculately encased by beautiful walls of shining white marble and was illuminated by a circle of light. In front of them, an enormous visual platform appeared above a control panel of some sort. To the right side stood a structure resembling a threshold or doorway. They were completely alone in the chamber. No other life entity was present.

Erica began to realize that this chamber truly was the archives of Atlantis. It was not at all what she had envisioned like the leather and papyrus scrolls were said to be kept in the Library of Alexandria. Sadly, that ancient record perished in the great fire. No, this place was worthy of an advanced civilization. Its history was stored in mega bites of computer language to preserve its record for millennia. It was here and it was safe from the environment and the uneducated masses that would follow the great destruction of their continent and its inhabitants.

The chamber was actually reverent and silent, except for an almost inaudible hum.

"Troy, do hear a slight sound, a steady hum of some kind?"

"I'm glad you asked. I hear something, just don't know where it's coming from. It seems to be all around us."

"Yes, perhaps some kind of solar energy powering the chamber. The sun is an endless source of energy. I believe the Atlanteans harnessed the sun to power this chamber for perpetuity, forever."

"Seems so, but what is the purpose of the strange threshold?"

Just then, Erica began to feel weak in the knees and insisted she needed to sit on the floor for a moment to think.

"You haven't read Casey. During his trances, he described time travel, that the Atlanteans had developed a way to travel back and forth through time." She studied the threshold and continued, "I think that is a portal to another time or dimension."

Troy let the thought mull around in his mind, then offered, "Do you think Maggie tried to go through the portal?"

She slowly nodded and said, "I think she did. Maybe that's why she looked as if she aged before she returned. The idea of time travel is exhilarating but also frightening. Who knows what could happen if that knowledge was misused for evil purposes by men with power. Case in point, the Atlanteans themselves. She knew it was dangerous, and the reason Maggie wrote 'tell no one'."

Yet, it was almost hypnotic, a mystery begging to be revealed. After all, she was following in her mother's footsteps. She rose to her feet and began moving toward the portal when Troy suddenly pulled her back.

"Erica no, please. Leave it alone. If you go, you might not come back at all," Troy pleaded with her, holding onto her hand. "Don't go; stay here where you belong, in this time. Stay with me, Erica."

He held her tightly and they embraced stronger and longer than they had ever before.

She looked around the chamber and nodded her

head. "Yes, we found what we came for. This place is not meant for the world we live in today. It is too dangerous. Our civilization is not ready for this kind of power or knowledge. It will most certainly be abused. The Atlanteans destroyed their own land and distorted the very nature of this planet. No one must know, no one, agreed?"

"I'm with you all the way, love. Thank you for staying." He kissed her softly, then added, "So let's find a way out of here."

Erica kissed him again and said, "Let's go."

She looked around the chamber, searching for something that would transport them outside again. She needed to be certain before touching anything that might trigger a bad outcome. The computer console was so inviting, but there was no way to know how it operated without touching it. No, it had to be something behind them. When they first arrived in the chamber, they were facing the console. Reasonable deduction suggested she needed to search the wall behind them.

"Troy, do you see anything similar to what we saw between the columns?"

"I remember you touching the center of a pyramid carving on the wall."

"Yes, then it must be the key."

Erica searched for a pyramid symbol and was surprised that it was so easily obvious. There, on the marble wall, was a perfect pyramid design with an eye at its center.

She held out her hand to Troy and said, "This must be it. Coming with me?"

Smiling, he took her hand and stood close to her. "Ready."

The moment she touched the eye, the dizzying sensation came over them, transporting them outside the wall again. They immediately sat down on the ledge and held each other until their heads cleared. The sun was close to the horizon now, and Troy's men still sat next to the camels below, waiting for their return.

He stood and looked down the hillside for a possible, safe way down. He knew going down would be easier than trying to climb up the hill. They needed fresh water and nourishment. The long trek back to the second marker would be too dangerous in the dark.

"Erica, do you trust me?"

"Of course I trust you, Troy."

"Then let's slowly slide down the hill to the others. It will be okay. We'll get pretty dirty, but we might make it back to camp before nightfall."

"Count me in, let's go."

They walked along the ledge until it ended and then began their descent. The limestone shifted and crumbled around them, but they managed to safely reach the dessert floor. Before dark, they joined the others, remounted, and headed for the camp. Erica couldn't wait to wash the dessert from her hair and body.

CHAPTER 8

Troy and Erica took turns pouring water over each other's naked bodies. They were filled with joy, and playfully danced around each other in the cooler night air, then took their time to dress. Troy put on a clean shirt and Erica slipped on her beautiful Kaftan.

They sat down by the lantern, had their meal and shared the honey liquor.

"What an incredible day. Thank you for saving me from myself," Erica said looking deeply into his eyes.

"I couldn't let you go through the portal. I was afraid it would hurt you," said Troy.

Erica looked skyward for a moment, realizing it meant the end of their journey.

"But we did it because of you; we did it."

Troy touched her shoulder and said, "I wouldn't have come at all if it hadn't been for you."

They both looked into the light of their lantern, silently searching for words.

Finally, Erica began, "So what now? Where do we go from here? Do we begin the trek back to Cairo in the morning?"

"Erica, I don't want to run the chance of endangering you while terrorists are operating in the Sahara. It's not safe and it would take too long. I'm going to put you on the Luxor train back to Cairo in the morning. You should get back to Grant by the end of the day."

"I see. I know you are right; it would be much safer. But I don't feel right about leaving you," said Erica.

"Grant will be waiting for you, won't he?" he asked.

"Yes, absolutely. He wouldn't leave me in Egypt alone."

"Good. When we get to the station tomorrow you can call him at the hotel to let him know you are on the way."

"Right. He will be so relieved to know I'm

coming back."

Troy took her hand in his and said, "We still have tonight."

"We do," she replied with a whisper.

Although they were fatigued by the exertion spent on the limestone all day, they turned off the lantern and laid down on the blanket once more.

Their mood was bittersweet, and their love making far less robust. They took time to touch and feel more deeply, slowly going through the motions under the crystal-clear night sky until they wrapped themselves in each other's arms. Sleep came quickly and the night passed them by.

They woke at early morning's light and silently watched the shadows on the limestone move across the hillside. The columns appeared, then vanished just as before. But the morning did not bring the promise of a new adventure. It was now more somber and their movements more robotic. They had a small breakfast, packed up for the short ride to Luxor, then set out again.

Luxor was not as active with tourists as it usually was; most of them left after the massacre. Military vehicles and soldiers were now present and on high alert for terrorist activity.

When they reached the station, Troy secured her passage on the train while Erica called Grant. He was elated to hear from her, and she was glad he had survived food poisoning.

As luck would have it, they arrived at the station just in time before the porter announced the boarding call. Troy and Erica stood together on the boarding platform and silently embraced one last time.

"Thank you for everything, Troy. Take care of Cleo for me."

It was an awkward remark, but she didn't know what else to say. She didn't want to leave him.

The porter loudly called for boarding again. With a heavy heart, Erica turned and stepped inside as the doors closed behind her. She then busied herself with finding her seat.

Troy had purchased a window seat for her. By the time she found it, she gladly sat down. She knew he and his team had most likely gone ahead, and she peered outside at the people busily going about their daily routines. It felt strange to be among civilization again after being in the Sahara for so long. She had been on a great journey of discovery, but that was now beginning to fade into the past. Even so, she was filled with a great sense of accomplishment while she looked out the window at the various stone works of antiquity in the distance.

Finally, the train pulled away from the station and began its trek to Cairo. She leaned against the window and closed her eyes for a moment until the shrill cry of a child reopened them. What she saw crushed her heart.

The train was passing Troy and his team moving along the road. They looked so small, so insignificant and antiquated from the train. Cleo dutifully followed behind the other camels without her rider. Then, Troy's face came into view. He looked sad and deflated, his head bowed.

Tears began streaming down Erica's face. What had meant everything to her, every waking moment of each day was now beginning to disappear from view. She had never felt such heartbreak in her life until that moment. She closed her eyes again and tried to shut out the world. The trip to Cairo would take all day.

Grant met her at the station later that night. Erica saw him standing at the platform when the train arrived.

"Erica, you look radiant; you look well, "he said

giving her a gentle hug. He looked closer and continued, "But there is something else, isn't there?"

"Thank you, Grant; you also look well. And yes, there is something else. I fell in love and now he's gone." A tear rolled down her cheek.

"And the archives?"

His question seemed so meaningless, but she responded, "Yes, we found it, and Maggie was right. No one must ever know."

Grant accepted her answer, knowing they would discuss it much later.

"We fly back to London tomorrow. Are you ready to go home?"

She nodded, overwhelmed with emotion and tears.

Grant gently consoled her as best as he could. He could see she was clearly distraught and not herself.

"You have indeed fallen in love, my dear. I can feel your pain. Come with me now, let's get you back to the hotel. You're worn out and it's late."

Two weeks after they returned to London, Erica learned she had been accepted as a prominent professional at the British Museum Department of

Antiquities. She was to report forthwith for indoctrination. It was a prestigious appointment that would provide certain advantages yet to come. She was gratefully honored since she had fiercely competed for the position.

But she just couldn't shake her melancholy. The position paled in comparison to the experience she encountered with Troy. He was in her thoughts during the day, and her body ached for him throughout each night. And even though she caressed herself trying to imagine his hands, his face, his body lying next to her, those desires remained unsatisfied, always ending alone, empty, and unfulfilled. Tears moistened her pillow every night. But work at the museum was always ongoing, so she forced herself to rest in order to carry on as the days passed.

As a new day began, she showered, dressed and prepared tea and scones before leaving for the museum. Birds were singing happily outside her window. She sat down and took her first sip of tea when there was a ring at her door.

When she opened the door, she was stunned into disbelief. Troy was standing in front of her.

"My God, Troy!"

She immediately threw her arms around him,

then stepped back again, "But how, how did you find me? I am beyond thrilled to see you!"

Troy gestured to a waiting car at the curb, "A certain Cambridge professor that we both know."

Erica looked at the car. Grant was smiling at the wheel. She threw her arms around Troy again, then stood back and said, "God bless Grant, but why, why are you here? What did you say to convince him?"

"I told him I wanted to make sure you are safe from haboobs in England," he answered with a big grin.

Erica burst into laughter, flashing an enormous smile that covered her face.

"Oh, I love you, Troy McCullum." She hugged him again and said, "I missed you so much. Tell me, how long can you stay? How long?"

Troy smiled back at her with hope in his eyes and said, "As long as you want me."

Erica leaped into his arms, with tears of joy running down her face. Then she looked to Grant waiting in the car and gestured to him, silently mouthing the words, "Thank you."

Grant gave her a quick wave and discretely drove away.

T. L. Conn is an American Author. She performed for many years as a theatrical actress and as a vocalist. She has now published several works of fiction. Visit her website at: tlconnbooks.com, for the latest news of available and upcoming publications.

EDITOR'S REVIEW

After reading the book I wondered what a masterpiece this book is. The characters are endearing and the plot is remarkable in its simplicity and nuance.